A Car T[

Story by Jenny Giles
Illustrations by Liz Alger

Rigby®
A Harcourt Achieve Imprint

www.Rigby.com
1-800-531-5015

James is in the car.

Kate is in the car.

Mom said,

"Come in the car, Nick."

"No, Mom! No!" said Nick.

Dad said,

"Come here, Nick!

Come in the car!"

"Here I come," said Nick.

"Look!" said Nick.

"Here is Teddy."

Mom is in the car.

Dad is in the car.

Nick is in the car.

15

And Teddy is in the car, too.